Snow on Bear's Nose

A story of a Japanese moon bear cub

told by JENNIFER BARTOLI

Illustrated by TAKEO ISHIDA

Albert Whitman & Company, Chicago

Albert Whitman Edition 1976 • Illustrations © 1972 Gakken Co., Ltd. • Printed in Japan

The wind blew leaves in golden circles around the bear family. It told of changes coming on their mountain.

The little cubs, Kuma Chan and Kumako Chan, played in the warm sunshine. They climbed wild vines to eat the sweet grapes.

The old mother bear felt the wind on her back. Winter was coming. But how could Kumako Chan and her brother know this?

The wind blew red and yellow leaves by the river, too. The river was full of good things bears like to eat. There were fish deep in the water, and river crabs that crawled sideways on the rocks.

But Kumako Chan did not hurry to eat. She played with the wind and the water and the leaves.

The fall days slowly changed. The nights grew long. The wind was cold. It made strange noises in the trees. The bears changed too. They were fat now, and their fur was thick.

One morning the cubs followed their mother down the mountain.
Under an old tree was the den where they had been born last
winter. Now on cold winter days they would sleep in it again.

But Kumako Chan wasn't sleepy. She sniffed the cold air outside.
She looked once more at her sleeping family.

Then she was gone.

For the first time in her life Kumako Chan was all alone.
Clouds pushed across the sun above the trees. The forest
seemed dark. Birch trees bent in the rushing wind. But the
wind didn't bother her. She somersaulted and tumbled in
the waving grass.

Kumako Chan stopped when she came to an open field. A few
trees stood in the gray winter light. Kumako Chan climbed one.
   In another tree, two birds rested. Kumako Chan's dark eyes
watched them. But a bear cannot see far. So Kumako Chan did not
see the high mountains or the snow that was falling on them.

The birds flew away, and Kumako Chan climbed down the tree.

Two deer watched her. She was coming to the river. Where were the fish and river crabs? Kumako Chan didn't see them. She didn't hear the water, splashing on the rocks.

Kumako Chan reached down with her paws. All at once she was sliding. She tried to turn back. Crack! The ice broke.

Shaking her wet fur, Kumako Chan headed for the forest again. She was wet and cold and hungry, too.

The little bear pushed her nose under bushes and dug with her claws under old vines and leaves. She only found a few seeds and dried grapes to eat.

In the quiet forest, a twig dropped beside her. She looked up in a tree. There sat a squirrel, nibbling a nut from its nest. Kumako Chan listened. She was still hungry.

Kumako Chan went far into the forest looking for food. As she moved, the moon rose in the sky. It shone through the trees.

An owl high on a branch watched Kumako Chan curl up on the cold ground under a pile of dry leaves. She was sleepy now.
But a strong cold wind came and blew off her warm cover.

Kumako Chan growled softly in her sleep.
Only the owl heard.

While Kumako Chan slept, something touched her nose. It fell
on the trees and the grass and the leaves all around her.

It was blowing in the cold air when Kumako Chan opened her
eyes. She blinked. The sky was bright. Her nose tickled. She
sniffed and put out her tongue. What was it?

Snow! And it fell so fast Kumako Chan could hardly walk in
it. She sat down to rest in a clump of green bamboo.

Suddenly she heard a sound.
Her snowy nose smelled something.

Slowly in the snow came Kumako Chan's mother. Her head down, the old bear was sniffing and grunting.

The two bears sniffed and held each other. Kumako Chan was already warmer.

Then back through the deep snow Kumako Chan followed
her mother to their den.

The wind had told of winter coming. The mother bear knew that. Now her little cub knew what the wind meant, too. Winter is the time for bears to sleep on cold days, safe in their dens.

Kumako Chan settled down beside her brother. She did not listen to the wind. She went to sleep.

One day, warm winds would wake her.
But now it was time for Kumako Chan to sleep.

About Bears . . .

The bears in this story are Asiatic black bears, sometimes called moon bears because of the white fur crescent on their chests. They are not as large as American black bears; an adult may be about five feet long and weigh perhaps 250 pounds.

The Asiatic black bear is found from Japan on the east to the borders of Iran on the west. These bears typically live in forest or brush country. They eat both plant and animal food, and their habits vary somewhat according to the particular habitat.

If winters are mild, these bears sleep for only short periods. In fact, bears in general (unlike bats and woodchucks) do not have a true hibernation. They may make nestlike beds of twigs and leaves, waking when the winter sun shines warmly on them.

Bears have rather poor eyesight, hear fairly well, and have a fine sense of smell. Their feet have strong, sharp claws which are used for climbing and digging. While most animals run on their toes, a bear puts its whole foot down. This gives the animal the clumsy gait that the word "bear-like" suggests to us. Unlike some other species, moon bears romp and somersault.

In Japanese stories, a little bear is often named Kuma (*Ku'-ma*) Chan, meaning little bear or Teddy Bear. The feminine is Kumako (*Kum'-ako*) Chan.

Second Printing 1978

Library of Congress Cataloging in Publication Data
Bartoli, Jennifer.
    Snow on bear's nose.
    The illustrations appeared in 1972 in Whuff wants to see winter, by A. K. Herring.
    SUMMARY: A Japanese moon bear cub explores the forest learning about winter while her mother and brother sleep.
    1. Bears—Legends and stories. [i. Bears—Fiction.
2. Winter—Fiction] I. Ishida, Takeo, 1922-
II. Herring, Ann King. Whuff wants to see winter.
III. Title.
PZ10.3.B285Sn   [E]   76-40261
ISBN 0-8075-7520-8 lib. bdg.